HANSEL AND GRETEL

AND OTHER SIBLINGS FORSAKEN IN FORESTS

Amelia Carruthers

ORIGINS OF FAIRY TALES
FROM AROUND THE WORLD

CONTENTS

An Introduction to

the Fairy Tale

Fairy Tales are told in almost every society, all over the globe. They have the ability to inspire generations of young and old alike, yet fail to fit neatly into any one mode of storytelling. Today, most people know these narratives through literary works or even film versions, but this is a far cry from the genre's early development. Most of the stories began, and are still propagated through oral traditions, which are still very much alive in certain cultures. Especially in rural, poorer regions, the telling of tales – from village to village, or from elder to younger, preserves culture and custom, whilst still enabling the teller to vary, embellish or adapt the tale as they see fit.

To provide a brief attempt at definition, a fairy tale is a type of short story that typically features 'fantasy' characters, such as dwarves, elves, fairies, giants, gnomes, goblins, mermaids, trolls or witches, and usually magic or enchantments to boot! Fairy tales may be distinguished from other folk narratives such as legends (which generally involve belief in the veracity of the events described) and explicitly moral tales, including fables or those of a religious nature. In cultures where demons and witches are perceived as real, fairy tales may merge into legends, where the narrative is perceived both by teller and hearers as being grounded in historical truth. However unlike legends and epics, they usually do not contain more than superficial references to religion and actual places, people, and events; they take place 'once upon a time' rather than in reality.

The history of the fairy tale is particularly difficult to trace, as most often, it is only the literary forms that are available to the scholar. Still, written evidence indicates that fairy tales have existed for thousands of years, although not perhaps recognized as a genre. Many of today's fairy narratives have evolved from centuries-old stories that have appeared, with variations, in multiple cultures around the world. Two theories of origins have attempted to explain the common elements in fairy tales across continents. One is that a single point of origin generated any given tale, which then spread over the centuries. The other is that such fairy tales stem from common human experience and therefore can appear separately in many different origins. Debates still rage over which interpretation is correct, but as ever, it is likely that a combination of both aspects are involved in the advancements of these folkloric chronicles.

Some folklorists prefer to use the German term *Märchen* or 'wonder tale' to refer to the genre over *fairy tale,* a practice given weight by the definition of Thompson in his 1977 edition of *The Folktale.* He described it as 'a tale of some length involving a succession of motifs or episodes. It moves in an unreal world without definite locality or definite creatures and is filled with the marvellous. In this never-never land, humble heroes kill adversaries, succeed to kingdoms and marry princesses.' The genre was first marked out by writers of the Renaissance, such as Giovanni Francesco Straparola and Giambattista Basile, and stabilized through the works of later collectors such as Charles Perrault and the Brothers Grimm. The oral tradition of the fairy tale came long before the written page however.

Tales were told or enacted dramatically, rather than written down, and handed from generation to generation. Because of this, many fairy tales appear in written literature throughout different cultures, as in *The Golden Ass,* which includes *Cupid and Psyche* (Roman, 100–200 CE), or the *Panchatantra* (India, 3rd century CE). However it is still unknown to what extent these reflect the actual folk tales even of their own time. The 'fairy tale' as a genre became popular among the French nobility of the seventeenth century, and among the tales told were the *Contes* of Charles Perrault (1697), who fixed the forms of 'Sleeping Beauty' and 'Cinderella.' Perrault largely laid the foundations for this new literary variety, with some of the best of his works including 'Puss in Boots', 'Little Red Riding Hood' and 'Bluebeard'.

The first collectors to attempt to preserve not only the plot and characters of the tale, but also the style in which they were told were the Brothers Grimm, who assembled German fairy tales. The Brothers Grimm rejected several tales for their anthology, though told by Germans, because the tales derived from Perrault and they concluded that the stories were thereby *French* and not *German* tales. An oral version of 'Bluebeard' was thus rejected, and the tale of 'Little Briar Rose', clearly related to Perrault's 'The Sleeping Beauty' was included only because Jacob Grimm convinced his brother that the figure of *Brynhildr*, from much earlier Norse mythology, proved that the sleeping princess was authentically German. The Grimm Brothers remain some of the best-known story-tellers of folk tales though, popularising 'Hansel and Gretel', 'Rapunzel', 'Rumplestiltskin' and 'Snow White.'

The work of the Brothers Grimm influenced other collectors, both inspiring them to collect tales and leading them to similarly believe, in a spirit of romantic nationalism, that the fairy tales of a country were particularly representative of it (unfortunately generally ignoring any cross-cultural references). Among those influenced were the Norwegian Peter Christen Asbjørnsen (*Norske Folkeeventyr*, 1842-3), the Russian Alexander Afanasyev (*Narodnye Russkie Skazki*, 1855-63) and the Englishman, Joseph Jacobs (*English Fairy Tales*, 1890). Simultaneously to such developments, writers such as Hans Christian Andersen and George MacDonald continued the tradition of penning original literary fairy tales. Andersen's work sometimes drew on old folktales, but more often deployed fairytale motifs and plots in new stories; for instance in 'The Little Mermaid', 'The Ugly Duckling' and 'The Emperor's New Clothes.'

Fairy tales are still written in the present day, attesting to their enormous popularity and cultural longevity. Aside from their long and diverse literary history, these stories have also been stunningly illustrated by some of the world's best artists – as the reader will be able to see in the following pages. The Golden Age of Illustration (a period customarily defined as lasting from the latter quarter of the nineteenth century until just after the First World War) produced some of the finest examples of this craft, and the masters of the trade are all collected in this volume, alongside the original, inspiring tales. These images form their own story, evolving in conjunction with the literary development of the tales. Consequently, the illustrations are presented in their own narrative sequence, for the reader to appreciate *in and of themselves*. An introduction to the 'Golden Age' can also be found at the end of this book.

THE HISTORY OF
HANSEL AND GRETEL

The story of *Hansel and Gretel*, as fairy tales go, has a reasonably short historical lineage. It belongs to a group of European tales especially prevalent in the Baltic regions, about children who outwit witches or ogres into whose hands they have involuntarily fallen. Such tales, where a family's offspring are abandoned (usually in the woods) are thought to have originated in the medieval period of the Great Famine (1315-1321), which drove many people to desperate deeds. Deserting children in the forest to die, or leaving them to fend for themselves was certainly not unknown during the Late Middle Ages – and it is no small coincidence that the children are starving when they discover the gingerbread house.

Besides highlighting the endangerment of children (as well as their own cleverness), the 'Hansel and Gretel' tales all share a preoccupation with food: the mother or stepmother wants to avoid hunger, while the witch lures children to eat her house of candy, so that she can eat them. The best known version of the story was published by the Brothers Grimm, as *Hänsel und Gretel* in their *Children's and Household Tales* (1812). For the Brothers Grimm, collecting tales of distinctly Germanic origin was a way of preserving their own cultural identity at a time when the French Emperor Napoleon was taking over vast swathes of Europe. This was part of a more general trend in the nineteenth century, whereby folk stories garnered substantial interest, seen to represent a pure form of national literature and culture; deriving from the common folk (*Volk*). Although the brothers gained a posthumous reputation for collecting their tales from peasants, many of the stories actually came from middle-class or aristocratic acquaintances. Some of their better known narratives (*Hänsel und Gretel* included) were narrated by Henriette Dorothea Wild, the well-respected daughter of a pharmacist. Dorothea, or *Dortchen* as she was known to the brothers, later became Wilhelm's wife.

In the Grimm's original 1812 version of the tale, both parents agreed to send the children into the woods, but by 1857 it was the wicked step-mother who came up with the plan. Although the Grimm's later story is the best known *Hansel and Gretel* plot today, a much earlier variant comes from Italy, penned by Giambattista Basile (1566 – 1632). Published posthumously, his fairy tale collection (*Il Pentamerone*) was in fact a key inspiration to the Brothers Grimm, who praised it highly as the first *national* collection of fairy tales. In *Nennillo e Nennella,* the cruel step-mother demands that the two children be put out of the house, but the father secretly leaves them a trail of oats, hoping they may find their way back. In a similar manner to the Grimm's later tale (where the children's breadcrumbs are eaten by birds), the father's plan is quashed when the oats are eaten by a donkey. This aspect, of young protagonists attempting to find their way home via a self-made trail, is prevalent in many other folk-tales. It is most notably found in Charles Perrault's *Petit Poucet* (1697) and Madame d'Aulnoy's *Finette Cendrilon* (1721) – both of which the Grimms identified as parallel stories. Despite these initial similarities though, both *Petit Poucet* and *Finette Cendrillon* diverge substantially as the narrative progresses.

What all of these early versions do have in common, is the basic aspect of *survival* – a remnant of the coming-of-age rite-of-passage extant in Proto-Indo-European culture. The family has a universal and basic role in all civilizations, and it is the breakdown of the traditional family unit that causes the problems in the *Hansel and Gretel* storyline. When economic hardship hits, the parents abandon their own children. Despite this initial abandonment, when the relatives are eventually reunited, peace and happiness once again return. This is a common theme to many fairy tales, for instance the *Cinderella* chronicle, where the young girl's faithfulness to her mother's legacy demonstrates the timeless virtue of loyalty to one's kin. Or, more perilously, in the *Little Red Riding Hood Story* where the young girl's failure to heed her parent's warning to stay on the forest path leads to disastrous results. Aside from this familial aspect, the forest was also an incredibly threatening place for early European societies. Although a source of food and shelter for many, it was also seen as a harbinger of magic and danger – a location where people normally did not travel.

This explains why in so many variants of the *Hansel and Gretel* story, the witch (or in some cases, the 'ogre') is found deep within the forest. In the Russian legend, *Baba Yaga* (written down in Blumenthal's *Russian Folktales,* 1903), the cannibalistic witch is also located in the mysterious woods. Correspondingly, in the Romanian tale of the *Little Boy and the Wicked Stepmother* (penned by Moses Gaster), the evil events also take place in the undergrowth. The Portuguese account of the *Two Children and the Witch* is the only exception (it is also the earliest variant, written down in 1882), with the children coming across the witch just off a road, *on the edge of the forest.* At the time of this story's genesis (around the fourteenth and fifteenth centuries), belief in witches was commonplace. Between 1500 and 1660, a staggering 80,000 suspected witches are thought to have been killed in Europe, with 80% of those put to death being women. The oven into which the witch is eventually relegated, is also redolent of the fires of hell as punishment for her sins. As is perhaps evident from these examples though, *Hansel and Gretel* has an unusually small geographic reach when compared to many other folkloric tales, with most versions coming from Europe.

There are legends from other cultures with striking similarities to the 'babes lost in the wood' narrative, including *Kadar and Cannibals* from Southern India, and *The Story of the Bird that Made Milk* from South Africa. Though they do differ substantially from the European narrative structures, the African tale is the most similar. Although it does not include a 'witch' character, magical animals provide the supernatural element. It tells the story of three children, banished by their father after letting his magical milk-producing bird loose. Similarly to the European tradition, the children's ostracisation is caused by the family's sudden loss of food, and they subsequently flee into the wilderness.

In an intriguing departure from the Grimm's version, though in a comparable manner to Basile's *Nennillo e Nennella,* the children do not return home, but enjoy lives of plenty – before eventually meeting their parents again. This time, the plot is reversed, and the children benevolently rescue the adults from a famine sweeping the country.

As a testament to this stories ability to inspire and entertain generations of readers, *Hansel and Gretel* continues to influence popular culture internationally, lending plot elements, allusions, and tropes to a wide variety of artistic mediums. It has been translated into almost every language, and very excitingly, is continuing to evolve in the present day. We hope the reader enjoys this collection of some of its best re-tellings.

Nennillo e Nennella

(An Italian Tale)

Nennillo e Nenella was written by Giambattista Basile (1566-1632), a Neapolitan poet and courtier. It was first published in his collection of Neapolitan fairy tales titled *Lo Cunto de li Cunti Overo lo Ttrattenemiento de Peccerille* (translating as 'The Tale of Tales, or Entertainment for Little Ones'), posthumously published in two volumes in 1634 and 1636.

Although neglected for some time, the work received a great deal of attention after the Brothers Grimm praised it highly as the first *national* collection of fairy tales. Many of the fairy tales that Basile collected are the oldest known variants in existence, including this – the oldest printed version of the *Hansel and Gretel* narrative. Unlike many later accounts, the siblings are separated after their ordeal in the woods, with one being rescued by a prince, and the other adopted by pirates...

Woe to him who thinks to find a governess for his children by giving them a stepmother! He only brings into his house the cause of their ruin. There never yet was a stepmother who looked kindly on the children of another; or if by chance such a one were ever found, she would be regarded as a miracle, and be called a white crow. But beside all those of whom you may have heard, I will now tell you of another, to be added to the list of heartless stepmothers, whom you will consider well deserving the punishment she purchased for herself with ready money.

The Wood-Cutter finds May Bird.
Popular Nursery Stories, 1919.
Illustrated by John Hassall

There was once a good man named Jannuccio, who had two children, Nennillo and Nennella, whom he loved as much as his own life. But Death having, with the smooth file of Time, severed the prison bars of his wife's soul, he took to himself a cruel woman, who had no sooner set foot in his house than she began to ride the high horse, saying, "Am I come here indeed to look after other folk's children? A pretty job I have undertaken, to have all this trouble and be for ever teased by a couple of squalling brats! Would that I had broken my neck ere I ever came to this place, to have bad food, worse drink, and get no sleep at night! Here's a life to lead! Forsooth I came as a wife, and not as a servant; but I must find some means of getting rid of these creatures, or it will cost me my life: better to blush once than to grow pale a hundred times; so I've done with them, for I am resolved to send them away, or to leave the house myself forever."

The poor husband, who had some affection for this woman, said to her, "Softly, wife! Don't be angry, for sugar is dear; and tomorrow morning, before the cock crows, I will remove this annoyance in order to please you."

So the next morning, ere the Dawn had hung out the red counterpane at the window of the East to air it, Jannuccio took the children, one by each hand, and with a good basketful of things to eat upon his arm, he led them to a wood, where an army of poplars and beech trees were holding the shades besieged.

Then Jannuccio said, "My little children, stay here in this wood, and eat and drink merrily; but if you want anything, follow this line of ashes which I have been strewing as we came along; this will be a clue to lead you out of the labyrinth and bring you straight home."

Then giving them both a kiss, he returned weeping to his house. But at the hour when all creatures, summoned by the constables of Night, pay to Nature the tax of needful repose, the two children began to feel afraid at remaining in that lonesome place, where the waters of a river, which was thrashing the impertinent stones for obstructing its course, would have frightened even a hero. So they went slowly along the path of ashes, and it was already midnight ere they reached their home.

When Pascozza, their stepmother, saw the children, she acted not like a woman, but a perfect fury; crying aloud, wringing her hands, stamping with her feet, snorting like a frightened horse, and exclaiming, "What fine piece of work is this? Is there no way of ridding the house of these creatures? Is it possible, husband, that you are determined to keep them here to plague my very life out? Go, take them out of my sight! I'll not wait for the crowing of cocks and the cackling of hens; or else be assured that tomorrow morning I'll go off to my parents' house, for you do not deserve me. I have not brought you so many fine things, only to be made the slave of children who are not my own."

Poor Jannuccio, who saw that matters were growing rather too warm, immediately took the little ones and returned to the wood; where giving the children another basketful of food, he said to them, "You see, my dears, how this wife of mine -- who is come to my house to be your ruin and a nail in my heart -- hates you; therefore remain in this wood, where the trees, more compassionate, will give you shelter from the sun; where the river, more charitable, will give you drink without poison; and the earth, more kind, will give you a pillow of grass without danger. And when you want food, follow this little path of bran which I have made for you in a straight line, and you can come and seek what you require."

So saying, he turned away his face, not to let himself be seen to weep and dishearten the poor little creatures.

The woodcutter climbed up, took the child down, and found it was a pretty little girl.
The Big Book of Fairy Tales, 1911.
Illustrated by Charles Robinson

Husband, listen to me.

Popular Nursery Stories, 1919.

Illustrated by John Hassall

When Nennillo and Nennella had eaten all that was in the basket, they wanted to return home; but alas! a jackass -- the son of ill-luck -- had eaten up all the bran that was strewn upon the ground; so they lost their way, and wandered about forlorn in the wood for several days, feeding on acorns and chestnuts which they found fallen on the ground.

But as Heaven always extends its arm over the innocent, there came by chance a prince to hunt in that wood. Then Nennillo, hearing the baying of the hounds, was so frightened that he crept into a hollow tree; and Nennella set off running at full speed, and ran until she came out of the wood, and found herself on the seashore. Now it happened that some pirates, who had landed there to get fuel, saw Nennella and carried her off; and their captain took her home with him where he and his wife, having just lost a little girl, took her as their daughter.

Meantime Nennillo, who had hidden himself in the tree, was surrounded by the dogs, which made such a furious barking that the prince sent to find out the cause; and when he discovered the pretty little boy, who was so young that he could not tell who were his father and mother, he ordered one of the huntsmen to set him upon his saddle and take him to the royal palace. Then he had him brought up with great care, and instructed in various arts, and among others, he had him taught that of a carver; so that, before three or four years had passed, Nennillo became so expert in his art that he could carve a joint to a hair.

Now about this time it was discovered that the captain of the ship who had taken Nennella to his house was a sea-robber, and the people wished to take him prisoner; but getting timely notice from the clerks in the law courts, who were his friends, and whom he kept in his pay, he fled with all his family. It was decreed, however, perhaps by the judgment of Heaven, that he who had committed his crimes upon the sea, upon the sea should suffer the punishment

Do not be afraid, Grethel, I will find some help for us.
The Big Book of Fairy Tales, 1911.
Illustrated by Charles Robinson

of them; for having embarked in a small boat, no sooner was he upon the open sea than there came such a storm of wind and tumult of the waves, that the boat was upset and all were drowned, all except Nennella, who having had no share in the corsair's robberies, like his wife and children, escaped the danger; for just then a large enchanted fish, which was swimming about the boat, opened its huge throat and swallowed her down.

The little girl now thought to herself that her days were surely at an end, when suddenly she found a thing to amaze her inside the fish: beautiful fields and fine gardens, and a splendid mansion, with all that heart could desire, in which she lived like a princess. Then she was carried quickly by the fish to a rock, where it chanced that the prince had come to escape the burning heat of a summer, and to enjoy the cool sea breezes. And whilst a great banquet was preparing, Nennillo had stepped out upon a balcony of the palace on the rock to sharpen some knives, priding himself greatly on acquiring honor from his office. When Nennella saw him through the fish's throat, she cried aloud,

> Brother, brother, your task is done,
> The tables are laid out every one;
> But here in the fish I must sit and sigh,
> Oh brother, without you I soon shall die.

Nennillo at first paid no attention to the voice, but the prince, who was standing on another balcony and had also heard it, turned in the direction whence the sound came, and saw the fish. And when he again heard the same words, he was beside himself with amazement, and ordered a number of servants to try whether by any means they could ensnare the fish and draw it to land.

At last, hearing the words "Brother, brother!" continually repeated, he asked all his servants, one by one, whether any of them had lost a sister. And

Nennillo replied, that he recollected, as a dream, having had a sister when the prince found him in the wood, but that he had never since heard any tidings of her. Then the prince told him to go nearer to the fish, and see what was the matter, for perhaps this adventure might concern him.

As soon as Nennillo approached the fish, it raised up its head upon the rock, and opening its throat six palms wide, Nennella stepped out, so beautiful that she looked just like a nymph in some interlude, come forth from that animal at the incantation of a magician. And when the prince asked her how it had all happened, she told him a part of her sad story, and the hatred of their stepmother; but not being able to recollect the name of their father nor of their home, the prince caused a proclamation to be issued, commanding that whoever had lost two children, named Nennillo and Nennella, in a wood, should come to the royal palace, and he would there receive joyful news of them.

Jannuccio, who had all this time passed a sad and disconsolate life, believing that his children had been devoured by wolves, now hastened with the greatest joy to seek the prince, and told him that he had lost the children. And when he had related the story, how he had been compelled to take them to the wood, the prince gave him a good scolding, calling him a blockhead for allowing a woman to put her heel upon his neck till he was brought to send away two such jewels as his children. But after he had broken Jannuccio's head with these words, he applied to it the plaster of consolation, showing him the children, whom the father embraced and kissed for half an hour without being satisfied.

Then the prince made him pull off his jacket, and had him dressed like a lord; and sending for Jannuccio's wife, he showed her those two golden pippins, asked her what that person would deserve who should do them any harm, and even endanger their lives.

Hansel picked up the glittering white pebbles and filled his pockets with them.
The Fairy Tales of the Brothers Grimm, 1909.
Illustrated by Arthur Rackham

And she replied, "For my part, I would put her into a closed cask, and send her rolling down a mountain."

"So it shall be done!" said the prince. "The goat has butted at herself. Quick now! you have passed the sentence, and you must suffer it, for having borne these beautiful stepchildren such malice."

So he gave orders that the sentence should be instantly executed. Then choosing a very rich lord among his vassals, he gave him Nennella to wife, and the daughter of another great lord to Nennillo; allowing them enough to live upon, with their father, so that they wanted for nothing in the world. But the stepmother, shut into the cask and shut out from life, kept on crying through the bunghole as long as she had breath:

> To him who mischief seeks, shall mischief fall;
> There comes an hour that recompenses all.

We are going into the wood.
The Big Book of Fairy Tales, 1911.
Illustrated by Charles Robinson

But Hansel lingered on and dropped the pebbles behind him.
Tales From Grimm, 1936.
Illustrated by Wanda Gag

HÄNSEL UND GRETEL

(A German Tale)

Hänsel und Gretel is a German tale written by the Brothers Grimm, (or *Die Brüder Grimm*), Jacob (1785–1863) and Wilhelm Grimm (1786–1859). It was first published in *Kinder und Hausmärchen* ('Children's and Household Tales') in 1812, although this particular version comes from the revised 1857 edition. *Kinder und Hausmärchen* was a pioneering collection of German folklore, and the Grimms built their anthology on the conviction that a national identity could be found in popular culture and with the common folk (*Volk*). Their first volumes were highly criticised however, because although they were called 'Children's Tales', they were not regarded as suitable for children, for both their scholarly information and gruesome subject matter.

Hänsel und Gretel was told to the Brothers Grimm by Henriette Dorothea Wild (who would later become Wilhelm's wife), and is reasonably similar to the Italian tale of *Nennillo e Nennella*. Most of the Grimms' stories were in fact based on pre-existing tales, but their flair for storytelling 'fixed' the narrative as we know it today. In Dortchen's original version, both the parents agreed to abandon Hänsel and Gretel, but with the Grimms' later revisions, the step-mother instigates the plan. The 'friendly duck' was also a new addition, as was the symbolic bone (representative of strength and permanence) which Hansel uses to trick the witch.

$$\rightarrow$$

Hard by a great forest dwelt a poor wood-cutter with his wife and his two children. The boy was called Hansel and the girl Gretel. He had little to bite and to break, and once when great dearth fell on the land, he could no longer procure even daily bread. Now when he thought over this by night in his bed, and tossed about in his anxiety, he groaned and said to his wife: 'What is to become of us? How are we to feed our poor children, when we no longer have anything even for ourselves?' 'I'll tell you what, husband,' answered the woman, 'early tomorrow morning we will take the children out into the forest to where it is the thickest; there we will light a fire for them, and give each of them one more piece of bread, and then we will go to our work and leave them alone. They will not find the way home again, and we shall be rid of them.' 'No, wife,' said the man, 'I will not do that; how can I bear to leave my children alone in the forest?—the wild animals would soon come and tear them to pieces.' 'O, you fool!' said she, 'then we must all four die of hunger, you may as well plane the planks for our coffins,' and she left him no peace until he consented. 'But I feel very sorry for the poor children, all the same,' said the man.

The two children had also not been able to sleep for hunger, and had heard what their stepmother had said to their father. Gretel wept bitter tears, and said to Hansel: 'Now all is over with us.' 'Be quiet, Gretel,' said Hansel, 'do not distress yourself, I will soon find a way to help us.' And when the old folks had fallen asleep, he got up, put on his little coat, opened the door below, and crept outside. The moon shone brightly, and the white pebbles which lay in front of the house glittered like real silver pennies. Hansel stooped and stuffed the little pocket of his coat with as many as he could get in. Then he went back and said to Gretel: 'Be comforted, dear little sister, and sleep in peace, God will not forsake us,' and he lay down again in his bed. When day dawned, but before the sun had risen, the woman came and awoke the two children, saying: 'Get up, you sluggards! we are going into the forest to fetch wood.' She gave each a little piece of bread, and said: 'There is something for your dinner, but do not eat it up before then, for you will get nothing else.' Gretel took the

Hansel and Grethel sat down by the fire.
My Book of Favourite Fairy Tales, 1921.
Illustrated by Jennie Harbour

bread under her apron, as Hansel had the pebbles in his pocket. Then they all set out together on the way to the forest. When they had walked a short time, Hansel stood still and peeped back at the house, and did so again and again. His father said: 'Hansel, what are you looking at there and staying behind for? Pay attention, and do not forget how to use your legs.' 'Ah, father,' said Hansel, 'I am looking at my little white cat, which is sitting up on the roof, and wants to say goodbye to me.' The wife said: 'Fool, that is not your little cat, that is the morning sun which is shining on the chimneys.' Hansel, however, had not been looking back at the cat, but had been constantly throwing one of the white pebble-stones out of his pocket on the road.

When they had reached the middle of the forest, the father said: 'Now, children, pile up some wood, and I will light a fire that you may not be cold.' Hansel and Gretel gathered brushwood together, as high as a little hill. The brushwood was lighted, and when the flames were burning very high, the woman said: 'Now, children, lay yourselves down by the fire and rest, we will go into the forest and cut some wood. When we have done, we will come back and fetch you away.'

Hansel and Gretel sat by the fire, and when noon came, each ate a little piece of bread, and as they heard the strokes of the wood-axe they believed that their father was near. It was not the axe, however, but a branch which he had fastened to a withered tree which the wind was blowing backwards and forwards. And as they had been sitting such a long time, their eyes closed with fatigue, and they fell fast asleep. When at last they awoke, it was already dark night. Gretel began to cry and said: 'How are we to get out of the forest now?' But Hansel comforted her and said: 'Just wait a little, until the moon has risen, and then we will soon find the way.' And when the full moon had risen, Hansel took his little sister by the hand, and followed the pebbles which shone like newly-coined silver pieces, and showed them the way.

Roland and Maybird in the depths of the wood.
Grimm's Fairy Tales, 1903.
Illustrated by Helen Stratton

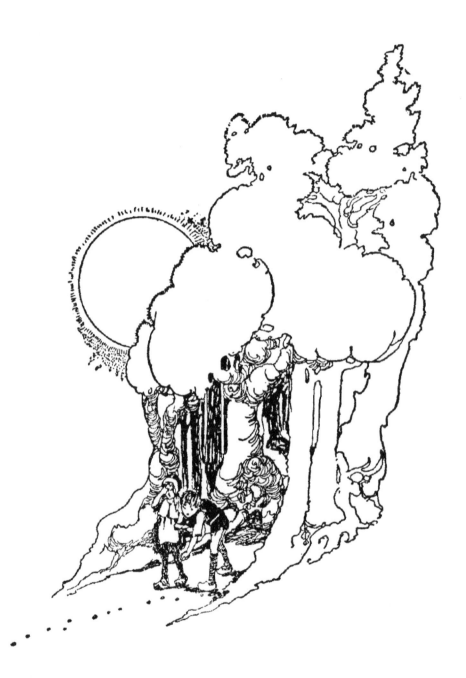

Hansel followed the pebbles.
The Fairy Tales of Grimm, 1936.
Illustrated by Anne Anderson

They walked the whole night long, and by break of day came once more to their father's house. They knocked at the door, and when the woman opened it and saw that it was Hansel and Gretel, she said: 'You naughty children, why have you slept so long in the forest?—we thought you were never coming back at all!' The father, however, rejoiced, for it had cut him to the heart to leave them behind alone.

Not long afterwards, there was once more great dearth throughout the land, and the children heard their mother saying at night to their father: 'Everything is eaten again, we have one half loaf left, and that is the end. The children must go, we will take them farther into the wood, so that they will not find their way out again; there is no other means of saving ourselves!' The man's heart was heavy, and he thought: 'It would be better for you to share the last mouthful with your children.' The woman, however, would listen to nothing that he had to say, but scolded and reproached him. He who says A must say B, likewise, and as he had yielded the first time, he had to do so a second time also.

The children, however, were still awake and had heard the conversation. When the old folks were asleep, Hansel again got up, and wanted to go out and pick up pebbles as he had done before, but the woman had locked the door, and Hansel could not get out. Nevertheless he comforted his little sister, and said: 'Do not cry, Gretel, go to sleep quietly, the good God will help us.'

Early in the morning came the woman, and took the children out of their beds. Their piece of bread was given to them, but it was still smaller than the time before. On the way into the forest Hansel crumbled his in his pocket, and often stood still and threw a morsel on the ground. 'Hansel, why do you stop and look round?' said the father, 'go on.' 'I am looking back at my little pigeon which is sitting on the roof, and wants to say goodbye to me,' answered Hansel. 'Fool!' said the woman, 'that is not your little pigeon, that is the morning sun that is shining on the chimney.' Hansel, however little by little, threw all the crumbs on the path.

Hansel, taking his sister's hand, followed the pebbles, which glittered like new-coined silver pieces.

My Book of Favourite Fairy Tales, 1921.

Illustrated by Jennie Harbour

The woman led the children still deeper into the forest, where they had never in their lives been before. Then a great fire was again made, and the mother said: 'Just sit there, you children, and when you are tired you may sleep a little; we are going into the forest to cut wood, and in the evening when we are done, we will come and fetch you away.' When it was noon, Gretel shared her piece of bread with Hansel, who had scattered his by the way. Then they fell asleep and evening passed, but no one came to the poor children. They did not awake until it was dark night, and Hansel comforted his little sister and said: 'Just wait, Gretel, until the moon rises, and then we shall see the crumbs of bread which I have strewn about, they will show us our way home again.' When the moon came they set out, but they found no crumbs, for the many thousands of birds which fly about in the woods and fields had picked them all up. Hansel said to Gretel: 'We shall soon find the way,' but they did not find it. They walked the whole night and all the next day too from morning till evening, but they did not get out of the forest, and were very hungry, for they had nothing to eat but two or three berries, which grew on the ground. And as they were so weary that their legs would carry them no longer, they lay down beneath a tree and fell asleep.

It was now three mornings since they had left their father's house. They began to walk again, but they always came deeper into the forest, and if help did not come soon, they must die of hunger and weariness. When it was mid-day, they saw a beautiful snow-white bird sitting on a bough, which sang so delightfully that they stood still and listened to it. And when its song was over, it spread its wings and flew away before them, and they followed it until they reached a little house, on the roof of which it alighted; and when they approached the little house they saw that it was built of bread and covered with cakes, but that the windows were of clear sugar. 'We will set to work on that,' said Hansel, 'and have a good meal. I will eat a bit of the roof, and you Gretel, can eat some of the window, it will taste sweet.' Hansel reached up above, and broke off a little of the roof to try how it tasted, and Gretel leant against the window and nibbled at the panes. Then a soft voice cried from the parlour:

'Nibble, nibble, gnaw,

Who is nibbling at my little house?'

The children answered:

'The wind, the wind,

The heaven-born wind,'

and went on eating without disturbing themselves. Hansel, who liked the taste of the roof, tore down a great piece of it, and Gretel pushed out the whole of one round window-pane, sat down, and enjoyed herself with it. Suddenly the door opened, and a woman as old as the hills, who supported herself on crutches, came creeping out. Hansel and Gretel were so terribly frightened that they let fall what they had in their hands. The old woman, however, nodded her head, and said: 'Oh, you dear children, who has brought you here? do come in, and stay with me. No harm shall happen to you.' She took them both by the hand, and led them into her little house. Then good food was set before them, milk and pancakes, with sugar, apples, and nuts. Afterwards two pretty little beds were covered with clean white linen, and Hansel and Gretel lay down in them, and thought they were in heaven.

The old woman had only pretended to be so kind; she was in reality a wicked witch, who lay in wait for children, and had only built the little house of bread in order to entice them there. When a child fell into her power, she killed it, cooked and ate it, and that was a feast day with her. Witches have red eyes, and cannot see far, but they have a keen scent like the beasts, and are

Oh Hansel, it's so dark!

Tales From Grimm, 1936.

Illustrated by Wanda Gag

aware when human beings draw near. When Hansel and Gretel came into her neighbourhood, she laughed with malice, and said mockingly: 'I have them, they shall not escape me again!' Early in the morning before the children were awake, she was already up, and when she saw both of them sleeping and looking so pretty, with their plump and rosy cheeks she muttered to herself: 'That will be a dainty mouthful!' Then she seized Hansel with her shrivelled hand, carried him into a little stable, and locked him in behind a grated door. Scream as he might, it would not help him. Then she went to Gretel, shook her till she awoke, and cried: 'Get up, lazy thing, fetch some water, and cook something good for your brother, he is in the stable outside, and is to be made fat. When he is fat, I will eat him.' Gretel began to weep bitterly, but it was all in vain, for she was forced to do what the wicked witch commanded.

And now the best food was cooked for poor Hansel, but Gretel got nothing but crab-shells. Every morning the woman crept to the little stable, and cried: 'Hansel, stretch out your finger that I may feel if you will soon be fat.' Hansel, however, stretched out a little bone to her, and the old woman, who had dim eyes, could not see it, and thought it was Hansel's finger, and was astonished that there was no way of fattening him. When four weeks had gone by, and Hansel still remained thin, she was seized with impatience and would not wait any longer. 'Now, then, Gretel,' she cried to the girl, 'stir yourself, and bring some water. Let Hansel be fat or lean, tomorrow I will kill him, and cook him.' Ah, how the poor little sister did lament when she had to fetch the water, and how her tears did flow down her cheeks! 'Dear God, do help us,' she cried. 'If the wild beasts in the forest had but devoured us, we should at any rate have died together.' 'Just keep your noise to yourself,' said the old woman, 'it won't help you at all.'

Early in the morning, Gretel had to go out and hang up the cauldron with the water, and light the fire. 'We will bake first,' said the old woman, 'I have already heated the oven, and kneaded the dough.' She pushed poor Gretel out

36

They could not find a path out of the wood.
The Blue Fairy Book, 1922.
Illustrated by H. J. Ford

Hansel and Grethel in the forest.
The Big Book of Fairy Tales, 1911.
Illustrated by Charles Robinson

to the oven, from which flames of fire were already darting. 'Creep in,' said the witch, 'and see if it is properly heated, so that we can put the bread in.' And once Gretel was inside, she intended to shut the oven and let her bake in it, and then she would eat her, too. But Gretel saw what she had in mind, and said: 'I do not know how I am to do it; how do I get in?' 'Silly goose,' said the old woman. 'The door is big enough; just look, I can get in myself!' and she crept up and thrust her head into the oven. Then Gretel gave her a push that drove her far into it, and shut the iron door, and fastened the bolt. Oh! then she began to howl quite horribly, but Gretel ran away and the godless witch was miserably burnt to death.

Gretel, however, ran like lightning to Hansel, opened his little stable, and cried: 'Hansel, we are saved! The old witch is dead!' Then Hansel sprang like a bird from its cage when the door is opened. How they did rejoice and embrace each other, and dance about and kiss each other! And as they had no longer any need to fear her, they went into the witch's house, and in every corner there stood chests full of pearls and jewels. 'These are far better than pebbles!' said Hansel, and thrust into his pockets whatever could be got in, and Gretel said: 'I, too, will take something home with me,' and filled her pinafore full. 'But now we must be off,' said Hansel, 'that we may get out of the witch's forest.'

When they had walked for two hours, they came to a great stretch of water. 'We cannot cross,' said Hansel, 'I see no foot-plank, and no bridge.' 'And there is also no ferry,' answered Gretel, 'but a white duck is swimming there: if I ask her, she will help us over.' Then she cried:

> 'Little duck, little duck, dost thou see,
> Hansel and Gretel are waiting for thee?
> There's never a plank, or bridge in sight,
> Take us across on thy back so white.'

A little bird sat there in a tree.
Tales From Grimm, 1936.
Illustrated by Wanda Gag

The duck came to them, and Hansel seated himself on its back, and told his sister to sit by him. 'No,' replied Gretel, 'that will be too heavy for the little duck; she shall take us across, one after the other.' The good little duck did so, and when they were once safely across and had walked for a short time, the forest seemed to be more and more familiar to them, and at length they saw from afar their father's house. Then they began to run, rushed into the parlour, and threw themselves round their father's neck. The man had not known one happy hour since he had left the children in the forest; the woman, however, was dead. Gretel emptied her pinafore until pearls and precious stones ran about the room, and Hansel threw one handful after another out of his pocket to add to them. Then all anxiety was at an end, and they lived together in perfect happiness. My tale is done, there runs a mouse; whosoever catches it, may make himself a big fur cap out of it.

*They came to a strange little hut, made of bread with a roof
of cake, and windows of barley-sugar.*

Grimm's Household Tales, 1912.

Illustrated by R. Anning Bell

THE TWO CHILDREN AND THE WITCH

(A Portuguese Tale)

This story comes from an anthology of *Portuguese Folk Tales*, compiled by Zófimo Consiglieri Pedroso (1851 – 1910), a Portuguese historian, writer, ethnographer and folklorist. He was devoted to the study of ethnography (the systematic study of people and cultures) and introduced anthropology as an academic pursuit to Portugal, studying the country's myths, popular traditions and superstitions. Ironically, for a book dedicated to Portuguese culture and story-telling, the book was actually issued in England (in 1878) *before* its native publication.

This particular tale is unusual in that the children are not purposely abandoned by their parents at all. In Pedroso's narrative, the mother merely sends the siblings to buy some beans – but on getting lost in the woods, they encounter the evil witch. In a corresponding manner to the Brothers Grimm's story, the manner of the witch's death demonstrates the enormity of her evil, thus upholding the tale's moral aspect.

➤——————→

There was once a woman who had a son and a daughter. The mother one day sent her son to buy five reis' worth of beans, and then said to both:

"My children, go as far out on the road as you shall find shells of beans strewed on the path, and when you reach the wood you will find me there collecting fire-wood."

The children did as they were bid; and after the mother had gone out they went following the track of the beans which she went strewing along the road, but they did not find her in the wood or anywhere else. As night had come on they perceived in the darkness a light shining at a distance, easy of access. They walked on towards it, and they soon came up to an old woman who was frying cakes. The old woman was blind of one eye, and the boy went on the blind side and stole a cake, because he felt so hungry. Believing that it was her cat which had stolen the cake, she said,

"You thief of a cat! leave my cakes alone; they are not meant for you!"

The little boy now said to his sister,

"You go now and take a cake."

But the little girl replied,

"I cannot do so, as I am sure to laugh."

Still, as the boy persisted upon it and urged her to try, she had no other alternative but to do so. She went on the side of the old woman's blind eye and stole another of her cakes. The old woman, again thinking that it was her cat, said,

"Be off! shoo you old pussy; these cakes are not meant for you!"

The little girl now burst out into a fit of laughter, and the old hag turning round then, noticed the two children, and addressed them thus:

"Ah! is it you, my dear grandchildren? Eat, eat away, and get fat!"

The cottage was made of bread and cakes.
My Book of Favourite Fairy Tales, 1921.
Illustrated by Jennie Harbour

She then took hold of them and thrust them into a large box full of chestnuts, and shut them up. Next day she came close to the box and spoke to them thus:

"Show me your little fingers, my pets, that I may be able to judge whether you have grown fat and sleek."

The children put out their little fingers as desired. But next day the old hag again asked them:

"Show your little fingers, my little dears, that I may see if you have grown fat and plump!"

The children, instead of their little fingers, showed her the tail of a cat they had found inside the box. The old hag then said:

"My pets, you can come out now, for you have grown nice and plump."

She took them out of the box, and told them they must go with her and gather sticks. The children went into the wood searching one way while the old hag took another direction. When they had arrived at a certain spot they met a fay. This fay said to them:

"You are gathering sticks, my children, to heat the oven, but you do not know that the old hag wants to bake you in it."

She further told them that the old witch meant to order them to stand on the baker's peel, but that they were to ask her to sit upon it herself first, that so they might learn the way to do it.

"It's the loveliest house I ever saw," Gasped Gretel.

Tales From Grimm, 1936.

Illustrated by Wanda Gag

They saw that the cottage was made of bread and cakes.
Hansel and Gretel and Other Stories, 1925.
Illustrated by Kay Nielsen

The fay then went away. Shortly after they had met this good lady they found the old witch in the wood. They gathered together in bundles all the fire-sticks they had collected, and carried them home to heat the oven. When they had finished heating the oven, the old hag swept it carefully out, and then said to the little ones,

"Sit here, my little darlings, on this peel, that I may see how prettily you dance in the oven!"

The children replied to the witch as the good fay had instructed them:

"Sit you here, little granny, that we may first see you dance in the oven."

As the hag's intention was to bake the children, she sat on the peel first, so as to coax them to do the same after her; but the very moment the children saw her on the peel they thrust the peel into the oven with the witch upon it. The old hag gave a great start, and was burnt to a cinder immediately after. The children took possession of the shed and all it contained.

They begin to eat the cake and the sugar.

Roland and Maybird and Other Stories from Grimm, 1906.

Illustrated by Helen Stratton

THE STORY OF THE BIRD
THAT MADE MILK

(An African Tale)

This story was written down by Georg McCall Theal, in *Kaffir Folk-Lore* (published 1886). Now an offensive ethnic slur, the word 'kaffir' was formerly used as a South-African term to refer to a black person. It originally derived from the Arabic term 'kafir', meaning 'infidel', but was appropriated by European explorers and traders in the eighteenth and nineteenth centuries. Theal himself was a journalist, publisher and historian of Canadian descent, living in South Africa.

Although this tale does not include the traditional 'witch' character, the magical animals provide the story's supernatural element. It differs strongly (as would be expected) from the European tradition of the *Hansel and Gretel* narrative, but does retain some remarkable similarities. The sibling's expulsion is caused by the family's sudden loss of food, after which the children are banished into the wilderness. In an intriguing departure from the Grimm's version, though in a comparable manner to Basile's *Nennillo e Nennella,* the children do not return home, but enjoy lives of plenty – before they eventually meet their long lost parents.

There was once upon a time a poor man living with his wife in a certain village. They had three children, two boys and a girl. They used to get milk from a tree. That milk of the tree was got by squeezing. It was not nice as that

51

of a cow, and the people that drank it were always thin. For this reason, those people were never glossy like those who are fat.

One day the woman went to cultivate a garden. She began by cutting the grass with a pick, and then putting it in a big heap. That was the work of the first day, and when the sun was just about to set she went home. When she left, there came a bird to that place, and sang this song:

> "Weeds of this garden,
> Weeds of this garden,
> Spring up, spring up;
> Work of this garden,
> Work of this garden,
> Disappear, disappear."

It was so.

The next morning, when she returned and saw that, she wondered greatly. She again put it in order on that day, and put some sticks in the ground to mark the place.

In the evening she went home and told that she had found the grass which she had cut growing just as it was before.

Her husband said: "How can such a thing be? You were lazy and didn't work, and now tell me this falsehood. just get out of my sight, or I'll beat you."

On the third day she went to her work with a sorrowful heart, remembering the words spoken by her husband. She reached the place and found the grass growing as before. The sticks that she stuck in the ground were there still, but she saw nothing else of her labour. She wondered greatly.

The door opened and a little old fairy came out.

The Big Book of Fairy Tales, 1911.

Illustrated by Charles Robinson

Suddenly opened the door.
Grimm's Fairy Tales, 1914.
Illustrated by Harry G. Theaker

She said in her heart, "I will not cut the grass off again, I will just hoe the ground as it is."

She commenced. Then the bird came and perched on one of the sticks.

It sang:

> "Citi, citi, who is this cultivating the ground of my father?
> Pick, come off;
> Pick handle, break;
> Sods, go back to your places!"

All these things happened.

The woman went home and told her husband what the bird had done. Then they made a plan. They dug a deep hole in the ground, and covered it with sticks and grass. The man hid himself in the hole, and put up one of his hands. The woman commenced to hoe the ground again. Then the bird came and perched on the hand of the man, and sang:

> "This is the ground of my father.
> Who are you, digging my father's ground?
> Pick, break into small pieces
> Sods, return to your places."

It was so.

Then the man tightened his fingers and caught the bird. He came up out of the place of concealment.

He said to the bird: "As for you who spoil the work of this garden, you will not see the sun any more. With this sharp stone I will cut off your head!"

Then the bird said to him: "I am not a bird that should be killed. I am a bird that can make milk."

The man said: "Make some, then."

The bird made some milk in his hand. The man tasted it. It was very nice milk.

The man said: "Make some more milk, my bird."

The bird did so. The man sent his wife for a milk basket. When she brought it, the bird filled it with milk.

The man was very much pleased. He said: "This pretty bird of mine is better than a cow."

He took it home and put it in a jar. After that he used to rise even in the night and tell the bird to make milk for him. Only he and his wife drank of it. The children continued to drink of the milk of the tree. The names of the children were Gingci, the first-born son; Lonci, his brother; and Dumangashe, his sister. That man then got very fat indeed, so that his skin became shining.

The girl said to her brother Gingci: "Why does father get fat and we remain so thin?"

He replied: "I do not know. Perhaps he eats in the night."

Suddenly the door opened, and an ancient dame leaning on a staff hobbled out.
A Child's Book of Stories, 1914.
Illustrated by Jessie Willcox Smith

All at once the door opened and an old woman, supporting
herself on a crutch, came hobbling out.

Hansel and Grethel and Other Tales, 1920.

Illustrated by Arthur Rackham

They made a plan to watch. They saw him rise in the middle of the night. He went to the big jar and took an eating mat off it. He said: "Make milk, my bird." He drank much. Again he said: "Make milk, my bird," and again he drank till he was very full. Then he lay down and went to sleep.

The next day the woman went to work in her garden, and the man went to visit his friend. The children remained at home, but not in the house. Their father fastened the door of the house, and told them not to enter it on any account till his return.

Gingci said: "To-day we will drink of the milk that makes father fat and shining; we will not drink of the milk of the euphorbia today."

The girl said: "As for me, I also say let us drink of father's milk to-day."

They entered the house. Gingci removed the eating mat from the jar, and said to the bird: "My father's bird, make milk for me."

The bird said: "If I am your father's bird, put me by the fireplace, and I will make milk."

The boy did so. The bird made just a little milk.

The boy drank, and said: "My father's bird, make more milk."

The bird said: "If I am your father's bird, put me by the door, then I will make milk."

The boy did this. Then the bird made just a little milk, which the boy drank.

Suddenly the door opened, and an ancient dame leaning on a staff hobbled out.
The Blue Fairy Book, 1922.
Illustrated by H. J. Ford

The girl said: "My father's bird, make milk for me."

The bird said: "If I am your father's bird, just put me in the sunlight, and I will make milk."

The girl did so. Then the bird made a jar full of milk.

After that the bird sang:

> "The father of Dumangashe came, he came,
> He came unnoticed by me.
> He found great fault with me.
> The little fellows have met together.
> Gingci the brother of Lonci.
> The Umkomanzi cannot be crossed,
> It is crossed by swallows
> Whose wings are long."

When it finished its song it lifted up its wings and flew away. But the girl was still drinking milk.

The children called it, and said: "Return, bird of our father," but it did not come back. They said, "We shall be killed to-day."

They followed the bird. They came to a tree where there were many birds.

The boy caught one, and said to it: "My father's bird, make milk."

It bled. They said. "This is not our father's bird."

This bird bled very much; the blood ran like a river. Then the boy released it, and it flew away. The children were seized with fear.

They said to themselves: "If our father finds us, he will kill us to-day."

In the evening the man came home. When he was yet far off, he saw that the door had been opened.

He said: "I did not shut the door that way."

He called his children, but only Lonci replied. He asked for the others.

Lonci said: "I went to the river to drink; when I returned they were gone."

He searched for them, and found the girl under the ashes and the boy behind a stone. He inquired at once about his bird. They were compelled to tell the truth concerning it.

Then the man took a riem and hung those two children on a tree that projected over the river. He went away, leaving them there. Their mother besought their father, saying that they should be released; but the man refused. After he was gone, the boy tried to escape. He climbed up the riem and held on to the tree; then he went up and loosened the riem that was tied to his sister. After that they climbed up the tree, and then went away from their home, They slept three times on the road.

They came to a big rock. The boy said

"We have no father and no mother; rock, be our house."

A very old woman, walking on crutches, came out.

Fairy Tales From Grimm, 1894.

Illustrated by Gordon Browne

The rock opened, and they went inside. After that they lived there in that place. They obtained food by hunting animals, they were hunted by the boy.

When they were already in that place a long time, the girl grew to be big. There were no people in that place. A bird came one day with a child, and left it there by their house.

The bird said: "So have I done to all the people."

After that a crocodile came to that place. The boy was just going to kill it, but it said: "I am a crocodile; I am not to be killed; I am your friend."

Then the boy went with the crocodile to the house of the crocodile, in a deep hole under the water.

The crocodile had many cattle and much millet. He gave the boy ten cows and ten baskets of millet.

The crocodile said to the boy You must send your sister for the purpose of being married to me."

The boy made a fold to keep his cattle in; his sister made a garden and planted millet. The crocodile sent more cattle. The boy made a very big fold, and it was full of cattle.

At this time there came a bird.

The bird said: "Your sister has performed the custom, and as for you, you should enter manhood."

Just then the door opened, and a very old woman walking upon crutches came out.
My Book of Favourite Fairy Tales, 1921.

Illustrated by Jennie Harbour

Just then the door opened, and a very old woman walking upon crutches came out.
The Arthur Rackham Fairy Book, 1933.
Illustrated by Arthur Rackham.

The crocodile gave one of his daughters to be the wife of the young man. The young woman went to the village of the crocodile, she went to be a bride.

They said to her: "Whom do you choose to be your husband?"

The girl replied: "I choose Crocodile."

Her husband said to her: "Lick my face."

She did so. The crocodile cast off its skin, and arose a man of great strength and fine appearance.

He said: "The enemies of my father's house did that; you, my wife, are stronger than they."

After this there was a great famine, and the mother of those people came to their village. She did not recognise her children, but they knew her and gave her food. She went away, and then their father came. He did not recognise them either, but they knew him. They asked him what he wanted. He told them that his village was devoured by famine. They gave him food, and he went away.

He returned again.

The young man said: "You thought we would die when you hung us in the tree."

He was astonished, and said: "Are you indeed my child?"

Crocodile then gave them [the parents] three baskets of corn, and told them to go and build on the mountains. He [the man] did so and died there on the mountains.

Come inside and I will give you a nice dinner.
Old, Old Fairy Tales, 1935.
Illustrated by Anne Anderson

BABA YAGA

(A Russian Tale)

Baba Yaga was written down by Verra Xenophontovna Kalamatiano de Blumenthal, in *Folk Tales from the Russian* (published in 1903). Despite this relatively recent publication, the first reference to 'Baba Yaga' occurs in 1755, with Mikhail V. Lomonosov's *Russian Grammar*. The Baba Yaga character (akin to the western European witch), tends to display a variety of typical attributes: a turning, chicken-legged hut, as well as a mortar, pestle, and/or mop or broom. She is also likely to mention the 'Russian scent' of those that visit her, and when inside of her dwelling, she is most often found stretched out over the stove, reaching from one corner of the hut to another.

Most of these intriguing characteristics are found in the tale below, pointing towards its uniquely Russian heritage. It contains the paradigm reference to the evil stepmother, along with the cannibalistic witch (of course, found deep within the woods). In a similar manner to the Portuguese variant, where a kindly fay gives the young children advice, the siblings receive counsel from their 'good old grandmother' with their escape aided (akin to the African and German accounts) by a magical animal.

Somewhere, I cannot tell you exactly where, but certainly in vast Russia, there lived a peasant with his wife and they had twins-son and daughter. One day the wife died and the husband mourned over her very sincerely for a long time. One year passed, and two years, and even longer. But there is no order in a house without a woman, and a day came when the man thought, "If I marry again possibly it would turn out all right." And so he did, and had children by his second wife.

The stepmother was envious of the stepson and daughter and began to use them hardly. She scolded them without any reason, sent them away from home as often as she wished, and gave them scarcely enough to eat. Finally she wanted to get rid of them altogether. Do you know what it means to allow a wicked thought to enter one's heart?

The wicked thought grows all the time like a poisonous plant and slowly kills the good thoughts. A wicked feeling was growing in the stepmother's heart, and she determined to send the children to the witch, thinking sure enough that they would never return.

"Dear children," she said to the orphans, "go to my grandmother who lives in the forest in a hut on hen's feet. You will do everything she wants you to, and she will give you sweet things to eat and you will be happy."

The orphans started out. But instead of going to the witch, the sister, a bright little girl, took her brother by the hand and ran to their own old, old grandmother and told her all about their going to the forest.

"Oh, my poor darlings!" said the good old grandmother, pitying the children, "my heart aches for you, but it is not in my power to help you. You have to go not to a loving grandmother, but to a wicked witch. Now listen to me, my darlings," she continued; "I will give you a hint: Be kind and good to everyone; do not speak ill words to any one; do not despise helping the weakest, and always hope that for you, too, there will be the needed help."

The old woman was a spiteful Fairy.
Popular Nursery Stories, 1919.
Illustrated by John Hassall

The good old grandmother gave the children some delicious fresh milk to drink and to each a big slice of ham. She also gave them some cookies-there are cookies everywhere-and when the children departed she stood looking after them a long, long time.

The obedient children arrived at the forest and, oh, wonder! there stood a hut, and what a curious one! It stood on tiny hen's feet, and at the top was a rooster's head. With their shrill, childish voices they called out loud:

"Izboushka, Izboushka! turn thy back to the forest and thy front to us!"

The hut did as they commanded. The two orphans looked inside and saw the witch resting there, her head near the threshold, one foot in one corner, the other foot in another corner, and her knees quite close to the ridge pole.

"Fou, Fou, Fou!" exclaimed the witch; "I feel the Russian spirit."

The children were afraid, and stood close, very close together, but in spite of their fear they said very politely:

"Ho, grandmother, our stepmother sent us to thee to serve thee."

"All right; I am not opposed to keeping you, children. If you satisfy all my wishes I shall reward you; if not, I shall eat you up."

Without any delay the witch ordered the girl to spin the thread, and the boy, her brother, to carry water in a sieve to fill a big tub. The poor orphan girl wept at her spinning-wheel and wiped away her bitter tears. At once all around her appeared small mice squeaking and saying:

"Mm! Mm! Mm! she said. They're mine for certain!"

Tales From Grimm, 1936.

Illustrated by Wanda Gag

We must run away quickly, for the old woman is a bad fairy, and will kill us.
The Big Book of Fairy Tales, 1911.
Illustrated by Charles Robinson

"Sweet girl, do not cry. Give us cookies and we will help thee."

The little girl willingly did so.

"Now," gratefully squeaked the mice, "go and find the black cat. He is very hungry; give him a slice of ham and he will help thee."

The girl speedily went in search of the cat and saw her brother in great distress about the tub, so many times he had filled the sieve, yet the tub was still dry. The little birds passed, flying near by, and chirped to the children:

"Kind-hearted little children, give us some crumbs and we will advise you."

The orphans gave the birds some crumbs and the grateful birds chirped again:

"Some clay and water, children dear!"

Then away they flew through the air.

The children understood the hint, spat in the sieve, plastered it up with clay and filled the tub in a very short time. Then they both returned to the hut and on the threshold met the black cat. They generously gave him some of the good ham which their good grandmother had given them, petted him and asked:

"Dear Kitty-cat, black and pretty, tell us what to do in order to get away from thy mistress, the witch?"

You must light the fire and fill the big pot with water and help me to make the breakfast.
Old, Old Fairy Tales, 1935.

Illustrated by Anne Anderson

"Well," very seriously answered the cat, "I will give you a towel and a comb and then you must run away. When you hear the witch running after you, drop the towel behind your back and a large river will appear in place of the towel. If you hear her once more, throw down the comb and in place of the comb there will appear a dark wood. This wood will protect you from the wicked witch, my mistress."

Baba Yaga came home just then.

"Is it not wonderful?" she thought; "everything is exactly right."

"Well," she said to the children, "today you were brave and smart; let us see to-morrow. Your work will be more difficult and I hope I shall eat you up."

The poor orphans went to bed, not to a warm bed prepared by loving hands, but on the straw in a cold corner. Nearly scared to death from fear, they lay there, afraid to talk, afraid even to breathe. The next morning the witch ordered all the linen to be woven and a large supply of firewood to be brought from the forest.

The children took the towel and comb and ran away as fast as their feet could possibly carry them. The dogs were after them, but they threw them the cookies that were left; the gates did not open themselves, but the children smoothed them with oil; the birch tree near the path almost scratched their eyes out, but the gentle girl fastened a pretty ribbon to it. So they went farther and farther and ran out of the dark forest into the wide, sunny fields.

The cat sat down by the loom and tore the thread to pieces, doing it with delight. Baba Yaga returned.

"Where are the children?" she shouted, and began to beat the cat. "Why hast thou let them go, thou treacherous cat? Why hast thou not scratched their faces?"

The cat answered: "Well, it was because I have served thee so many years and thou hast never given me a bite, while the dear children gave me some good ham."

The witch scolded the dogs, the gates, and the birch tree near the path.

"Well," barked the dogs, "thou certainly art our mistress, but thou hast never done us a favor, and the orphans were kind to us."

The gates replied:

"We were always ready to obey thee, but thou didst neglect us, and the dear children smoothed us with oil."

The birch tree lisped with its leaves, "Thou hast never put a simple thread over my branches and the little darlings adorned them with a pretty ribbon."

Baba Yaga understood that there was no help and started to follow the children herself. In her great hurry she forgot to look for the towel and the comb, but jumped astride a broom and was off. The children heard her coming and threw the towel behind them. At once a river, wide and blue, appeared and watered the field. Baba Yaga hopped along the shore until she finally found a shallow place and crossed it.

Again the children heard her hurry after them and so they threw down the comb. This time a forest appeared, a dark and dusky forest in which the roots were interwoven, the branches matted together, and the tree-tops touching

Put out your forefinger.
European Folk and Fairy Tales, 1913.
Illustrated by John D. Batten

each other. The witch tried very hard to pass through, but in vain, and so, very, very angry, she returned home.

The orphans rushed to their father, told him all about their great distress, and thus concluded their pitiful story:

"Ah, father dear, why dost thou love us less than our brothers and sisters?"

The father was touched and became angry. He sent the wicked stepmother away and lived a new life with his good children. From that time he watched over their happiness and never neglected them any more.

How do I know this story is true?

Why, one was there who told me about it.

Hansel put out a knuckle-bone, and the old woman, whose eyes were dim, could not see, and thought it was his finger, and she was astonished that he did not get fat.

Hansel and Grethel and Other Tales, 1920.

Illustrated by Arthur Rackham

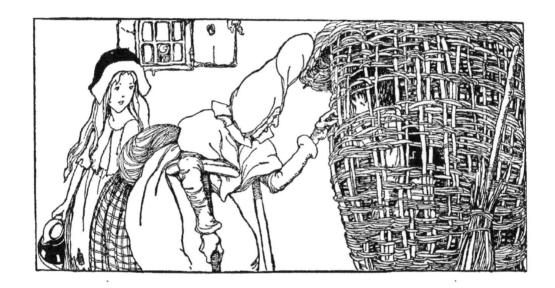

The old woman wondered very much that he did not get more fat.
The Fairy Tales of Grimm, 1936.
Illustrated by Anne Anderson

THE LITTLE BOY AND THE WICKED STEP-MOTHER

(A Romanian Tale)

The Story of the Little Boy and the Wicked Step-Mother comes from Moses Gaster's *Rumanian Bird and Beast Stories* (published in 1915). Gaster (1856 – 1939) was a Romanian-born Jewish-British scholar, a great collector of manuscripts and a member of the London Folk-Lore society. After being expelled from his homeland in 1885 (for alleged involvement with an irredentist society) he travelled to England where he lectured on Slavonic literature at the University of Oxford.

This particular story merges two tale types; type 327A (Hansel and Gretel), with type 720 (The Juniper Tree). The *Hansel and Gretel* aspect comes from the step-mother character insisting on the children's expulsion into the forest, as well as the sibling's attempts to find their way home via a dropped trail of ashes. It diverts in the latter half however, with the evil actions not committed by a witch, but by the step-mother herself. Like Jacob and Wilhelm Grimm's version of *The Juniper Tree,* the magical tree in this story enables the young child's eventual triumph.

⇒⟶

Once upon a time there was a poor man, who had a wife and two children, a boy and a girl. He was so poor that he possessed nothing in the world but the ashes on his hearth.

She thought it really was his finger, and wondered why it was that he did not get fat.
Tales From Grimm, 1936.
Illustrated by Wanda Gag

His wife died, and after a time he married another woman, who was cantankerous and bad natured, and from morning till evening, as long as the day lasted, she gave the poor man no peace, but snarled and shouted at him.

The woman said to him, "Do away with these children. You cannot even keep me. How then can you keep all these mouths?" for was she not a stepmother?

The poor man stood her nagging for a long time, but then, one night, she quarreled so much that he promised her that he would take the children into the forest and leave them there. The two children were sitting in the corner but held their peace and heard all that was going on.

The next day, the man, taking his axe upon his shoulder, called to the children and said to them, "Come with me into the forest. I am going to cut wood."

The little children went with him, but before they left, the little girl filled her pocket with ashes from the hearth, and as she walked along she dropped little bits of coal the way they went.

After a time they reached a very dense part of the forest, where they could not see their way any longer, and there the man said to the children, "Wait here for a while. I am only going to cut wood yonder. When I have done I will come back and fetch you home." And leaving the children there in the thicket, he went away, heavy hearted, and returned home.

The children waited for a while, and seeing that their father did not return, the girl knew what he had done. So they slept through the night in the forest, and the next morning, taking her brother by the hand, she followed the trace of the ashes which she had left on the road, and thus came home to their own house.

When the stepmother saw them, she did not know what to do with herself. She went almost out of her mind with fury. If she could, she would have swallowed them in a spoonful of water, so furious was she.

The husband, who was a weakling, tried to pacify her, and to endeavour to get the children away by one means or another, but did not succeed.

When the stepmother found that she could not do anything through her husband, she made up her mind that she herself would get rid of them. So one morning, when her husband had gone away, she took the little boy, and without saying anything to anybody, she killed him and gave him to his sister to cut him up, and prepare a meal for all of them. What was she to do? If she was not to be killed like her brother, she had to do what her stepmother told her.

And so she cut him up and cooked him ready for the meal But she took the heart, and hid it away in a hollow of a tree. When the stepmother asked her where the heart was, she said that a dog had come and taken it away.

In the evening, when the husband came home, she brought the broth with the meat for the husband to eat, and she sat down and ate of it, and so did the husband, not knowing that he was eating the flesh of his child. The little girl refused to eat it. She would not touch it. After they had finished, she gathered up all the little bones and hid them in the hollow of the tree where she had put the heart.

The next morning, out of that hollow of the tree there came a little bird with dark feathers, and sitting on the branch of a tree, began to sing, "Cuckoo! My sister has cooked me, and my father has eaten me, but I am now a cuckoo and safe from my stepmother."

"Creep in," said the Witch, "and see if it is properly hot."
Grimm's Fairy Tales, 1917.
Illustrated by Louis Rhead

'Stupid goose!' cried the witch. 'The opening is big enough:
you can see that I could get into it myself.'

Hansel and Grethel and Other Tales, 1920.

Illustrated by Arthur Rackham

When the stepmother, who happened to be near the tree, heard what that little bird was singing, in her fury and fright she took a heavy lump of salt which lay near at hand, and threw it at the cuckoo. But instead of hitting it, the lump fell down on her head and killed her on the spot.

And the little boy has remained a cuckoo to this very day.

The duck said "Quack! Quack!" and shook its head.
European Folk and Fairy Tales, 1913.
Illustrated by John D. Batten

JOHNNIE AND GRIZZLE

(An English Tale)

Johnnie and Grizzle was published by Joseph Jacobs (1854 – 1916), in his collection of *European Folk and Fairy Tales* (1916). This particular version of the narrative is almost identical to the Grimm's *Hänsel und Gretel*. Jacobs was greatly inspired by the work of the German antiquarians and the romantic nationalism common to folklorists of his age. He wished English children to have access to English fairy tales (despite this particular story originating from the Baltic States!). Jacobs felt that children were too focused on French and German stories, in his own words, 'What Perrault began, the Grimms completed.'

Apart from the anglicised names of 'Johnnie' and 'Grizzle' the tale remains relatively unchanged from the German version. One interesting derivation though, is Grizzle calling the witch character 'Mum.' This detail is not evidenced in any other tales. The closest parallel is the Russian story of *Baba Yaga*, where the witch is the children's step-grandmother. The reference to a mother figure perhaps links the character of the witch with the children's actual mother – who forsakes her offspring and thus suffers a terrible fate.

⮞——⟶

There was once a poor farmer who had two children named Johnnie and Grizzle. Now things grew worse and worse for the farmer till he could scarcely earn enough to eat and drink. All his crops went to pay rent and taxes. So one night he said to his wife,

91

Betty, my dear, I really do not know what to do; there is scarcely anything in the house to eat, and in a few days we shall all be starving. What I think of doing is to take the poor lad and lassie into the forest and leave them there; if somebody finds them they will surely keep them alive, and if nobody finds them they might as well die there as here; I cannot see any other way; it is their lives or ours; and if we die what can become of them?"

"No, no, father," said the farmer's wife; "wait but a few days and perhaps something will turn up.

"We have waited and have waited and things are getting worse every day; if we wait much longer we shall all be dead. No, I am determined on it; tomorrow the children to the forest."

Now it happened that Johnnie was awake in the next room and heard his father and his mother talking. He said nothing but thought and thought and thought; and early next morning he went out and picked a large number of bright colored pebbles and put them in his pocket. After breakfast, which consisted of bread and water, the farmer said to Johnnie and Grizzle, "Come, my dears, I am going to take you for a walk," and with that he went with them into the forest nearby.

Johnnie said nothing, but dropped one of his pebbles at every turning, which would show him the way back. When they got far into the forest the farmer said to the children, "My dears, I have to go and get something. Stay here and don't go away, and I'll soon come back. Give me a kiss, children, " and with that he hurried away and went back home by another road.

After a time Grizzle began to cry and said,

"Where's father? Where's father? We can't get home. We can't get home."

She shall take us over one at a time.

My Book of Favourite Fairy Tales, 1921.

Illustrated by Jennie Harbour

The swan would not near.
Popular Nursery Stories, 1919.
Illustrated by John Hassall

But Johnnie said, "Never mind, Grizzle, I can take you home; you just follow me."

So Johnnie looked out for the pebbles he had dropped, and found them at each turn of the road, and a little after midday got home and asked their mother for their dinner.

"There's nothing in the house, children, but you can go and get some water from the well and, please God, we'll have bread in the morning."

When the farmer came home he was astonished to find that the children had found their way home, and could not imagine how they had alone so. But at night he said to his wife, "Betty, my dear, I do not know how the children came home; but that does not make any difference; I cannot bear to see them starve before my eyes, better that they should starve in the forest. I will take them there again tomorrow."

Johnnie heard all this and crept downstairs and put some more pebbles into his pocket; and though the farmer took them this time further into the forest the same thing occurred as the day before. But this time Grizzle said to her mother and father, "Johnnie did such a funny thing; whenever we turned a new road he dropped pebbles. Wasn't that funny? And when we came back he looked for the pebbles, and there they were; they had not moved."

Then the farmer knew how he had been done, and as evening came on he locked all the doors so that Johnnie could not get out to get any pebbles. In the morning he gave them a hunk of bread as before for their breakfast and told them he was going to take them into the nice forest again. Grizzle ate her bread, but Johnnie put his into his pocket, and when they got inside the forest at every turning he dropped a few crumbs of his bread. When his father left them he tried to trace his way back by means of these crumbs. But, alas, and

Float, swan, float! Be our little boat.
Tales From Grimm, 1936.
Illustrated by Wanda Gag

alackaday! The little birds had seen the crumbs and eaten them all up, and when Johnnie went to search for them they had all disappeared.

So they wandered and they wandered, more and more hungry all the time, till they came to a glade in which there was a funny little house; and what do you think it was made of? The door was made of butterscotch, the windows of sugar candy, the bricks were all chocolate creams, the pillars of lollipops, and the roof of gingerbread.

No sooner had the children seen this funny little house than they rushed up to it and commenced to pick pieces off the door, and take out some of the bricks, while Johnnie climbed on Grizzly's back, and tore off some of the roof (what was that made of?). Just as they were eating all this the door opened and a little old woman, with red eyes, came out and said, "Naughty, naughty children to break up my house like that. Why didn't you knock at the door and ask to have something, and I would gladly give it to you?"

"Please ma'am," said Johnnie, "I will ask for something; I am so, so hungry, or else I wouldn't have hurt your pretty roof." "Come inside my house," said the old woman and let them come into her parlour. And that was made all of candies, the chairs and table of maple sugar, and the couch of coconut. But as soon as the old woman got them inside her door she seized hold of Johnnie and took him through the kitchen and put him in a dark cubby-hole, and left him there with the door locked.

Now this old woman was a witch, who looked out for little children, whom she fattened up and ate. So she went back to Grizzle, and said, "You shall be my little servant and do my work for me, and, as for that brother of yours, he'll make a fine meal when he's fattened up." So this witch kept Johnnie and Grizzle with her, making Grizzle do all the housework, and every morning she went to the cubby-hole in which she kept Johnnie and gave him a good breakfast, and later in the day a good dinner, and at night a good supper; but after she gave him his supper she would say to him, "Put out your forefinger," and when he put it out the old witch, who was nearly blind, felt it and muttered, "Not fat enough yet!"

After a while Johnnie felt he was getting real fat and was afraid the witch would eat him up. So he searched about till he found a stick about the size of his finger, and when the old witch asked him to put out his finger he put out the stick, and she said, "Goodness gracious me, the boy is as thin as a lath! I must feed him up more."

So she gave him more and more food, and every day he put out the stick till at last one day he got careless, and when she took the stick it fell out of his hand, and she felt what it was. So she flew into a terrible rage and called out, "Grizzle, Grizzle, make the oven hot. This lad is fat enough for Christmas."

Poor Grizzle did not know what to do, but she had to obey the witch. So she piled the wood on under the oven and set it alight. And after a while the old witch said to her,

"Grizzle, Grizzle, is the oven hot?" And Grizzle said, "I don't know, mum."

And when the witch asked her again whether it was hot enough, Grizzle said, "I do not know how hot an oven ought to be." "Get away, get away," said the old witch; "I know, let me see." And she poked her old head into the oven. Then Grizzle pushed her right into the oven and closed the door and rushed out into the back yard and let Johnnie out of the cubby-hole.

Then Johnnie and Grizzle ran away towards the setting sun where they knew their own house was, till at last they came to a broad stream too deep for them to wade. But just at that moment they looked back, and what do

Duck, Duck, here we stand.
Grimm's Fairy Tales, 1917.
Illustrated by Louis Rhead

Grethel shook her apron, and the pearls and precious stones rolled out upon the floor.
The Fairy Tales of Grimm, 1936.
Illustrated by Anne Anderson

you think they saw? The old witch, by some means or other, had got out of the oven and was rushing after them. What were they to do? What were they to do? Suddenly Grizzle saw a fine big duck swimming towards them, and she called out:

> "Duck, duck, come to me,
> Johnnie and Grizzle depend upon thee;
> Take Johnnie and Grizzle on thy back,
> Or else they'll be eaten—"

Arid the duck said:

"Quack! Quack!"

Then the duck came up to the bank, and Johnnie and Grizzle went into the water and, by resting their hands on the duck's back, swam across the stream just as the old witch came up.

At first she tried to make the duck come over and carry her, but the duck said, "Quack! Quack!" and shook its head.

Then she lay down and commenced swallowing up the stream, so that it should run dry and she could get across. She drank, and she drank, and she drank, and she drank, till she drank so much that she burst!

So Johnnie and Grizzle ran back home, and when they got there they found that their father the farmer had earned a lot of money and had been searching and searching for them over the forest, and was mighty glad to get back Johnnie and Grizzle again.

THE GOLDEN AGE OF ILLUSTRATION

The 'Golden age of Illustration' refers to a period customarily defined as lasting from the latter quarter of the nineteenth century until just after the First World War. In this period of no more than fifty years the popularity, abundance and most importantly the unprecedented upsurge in quality of illustrated works marked an astounding change in the way that publishers, artists and the general public came to view this hitherto insufficiently esteemed art form.

Until the latter part of the nineteenth century, the work of illustrators was largely proffered anonymously, and in England it was only after Thomas Bewick's pioneering technical advances in wood engraving that it became common to acknowledge the artistic and technical expertise of book and magazine illustrators. Although widely regarded as the patriarch of the *Golden Age*, Walter Crane (1845-1915) started his career as an anonymous illustrator – gradually building his reputation through striking designs, famous for their sharp outlines and flat tints of colour. Like many other great illustrators to follow, Crane operated within many different mediums; a lifelong disciple of William Morris and a member of the Arts and Crafts Movement, he designed all manner of objects including wallpaper, furniture, ceramic ware and even whole interiors. This incredibly important and inclusive phase of British design proved to have a lasting impact on illustration both in the United Kingdom and Europe as well as America.

The artists involved in the Arts and Crafts Movement attempted to counter the ever intruding Industrial Revolution (the first wave of which lasted roughly from 1750-1850) by bringing the values of beautiful and inventive craftsmanship back into the sphere of everyday life. It must be noted that around the turn of the century the boundaries between what would today be termed 'fine art' as opposed to 'crafts' and 'design' were far more fluid and in many cases non-operational, and many illustrators had lucrative painterly careers in addition to their design work. The Romanticism of the *Pre Raphaelite Brotherhood* combined with the intricate curvatures of the *Art Nouveaux* movement provided influential strands running through most illustrators work. The latter especially so for the Scottish illustrator Anne Anderson (1874-1930) as well as the Dutch artist Kay Nielson (1886-1957), who was also inspired by the stunning work of Japanese artists such as Hiroshige.

One of the main accomplishments of nineteenth century illustration lay in its ability to reach far wider numbers than the traditional 'high arts'. In 1892 the American critic William A. Coffin praised the new medium for popularising art; 'more has been done through the medium of illustrated literature... to make the masses of people realise that there is such a thing as art and that it is worth caring about'. Commercially, illustrated publications reached their zenith with the burgeoning 'Gift Book' industry which emerged in the first decade of the twentieth century. The first widely distributed gift book was published in 1905. It comprised of Washington Irving's short story *Rip Van Winkle* with the addition of 51 colour plates by a true master of illustration; Arthur Rackham. Rackham created each plate by first painstakingly drawing his subject in a sinuous pencil line before applying an ink layer – then he used layer upon layer of delicate watercolours to build up the romantic yet calmly ethereal results on which his reputation was constructed. Although Rackham is now one of the most recognisable names in illustration, his delicate palette owed no small debt to Kate Greenaway (1846-1901) – one of the first female illustrators whose pioneering and incredibly subtle use of the watercolour medium resulted in her election to the Royal Institute of Painters in Water Colours in 1889.

The year before Arthur Rackam's illustrations for *Rip Van Winkle* were published, a young and aspiring French artist by the name of Edmund Dulac

(1882-1953) came to London and was to create a similarly impressive legacy. His timing could not have been more fortuitous. Several factors converged around the turn of the century which allowed illustrators and publishers alike a far greater freedom of creativity than previously imagined. The origination of the 'colour separation' practice meant that colour images, extremely faithful to the original artwork could be produced on a grand scale. Dulac possessed a rigorously painterly background (more so than his contemporaries) and was hence able to utilise the new technology so as to allow the colour itself to refine and define an object as opposed to the traditional pen and ink line. It has been estimated that in 1876 there was only one 'colour separation' firm in London, but by 1900 this number had rocketed to fifty. This improvement in printing quality also meant a reduction in labour, and coupled with the introduction of new presses and low-cost supplies of paper this meant that publishers could for the first time afford to pay high wages for highly talented artists.

Whilst still in the U.K, no survey of the *Golden Age of Illustration* would be complete without a mention of the Heath-Robinson brothers. Charles Robinson was renowned for his beautifully detached style, whether in pen and ink or sumptuous watercolours. Whilst William (the youngest) was to later garner immense fame for his carefully constructed yet tortuous machines operated by comical, intensely serious attendants. After World War One the Robinson brothers numbered among the few artists of the Golden Age who continued to regularly produce illustrated works. As we move towards the United States, one illustrator - Howard Pyle (1853-1911) stood head and shoulders above his contemporaries as the most distinguished illustrator of the age. From 1880 onwards Pyle illustrated over 100 volumes, yet it was not quantity which ensured his precedence over other American (and European) illustrators, but quality.

Pyle's sumptuous illustrations benefitted from a meticulous composition process livened with rich colour and deep recesses, providing a visual framework n which tales such as *Robin Hood* and *The Four Volumes of the Arthurian Cycle* could come to life. These are publications which remain continuous good sellers up till the present day. His flair and originality combined with a thoroughness of planning and execution were principles which he passed onto his many pupils at the *Drexel Institute of Arts and Sciences*. Two such pupils were Jessie Willcox Smith (1863-1935) who went on to illustrate books such as *The Water Babies* and *At the Back of North Wind* and perhaps most famously Maxfield Parrish (1870-1966) who became famed for luxurious colour (most remarkably demonstrated in his blue paintings) and imaginative designs; practices in no short measure gleaned from his tutor. As an indication of Parrish's popularity, in 1925 it was estimated that one fifth of American households possessed a Parrish reproduction.

As is evident from this brief introduction to the 'Golden Age of Illustration', it was a period of massive technological change and artistic ingenuity. The legacy of this enormously important epoch lives on in the present day – in the continuing popularity and respect afforded to illustrators, graphic and fine artists alike. This *Origins of Fairy Tales from Around the World* series will hopefully provide a fascinating insight into an era of intense historical and creative development, bringing both little known stories, and the art that has accompanied them, back to life.

Other titles in the 'Origins of
Fairy Tales from Around the World' series...

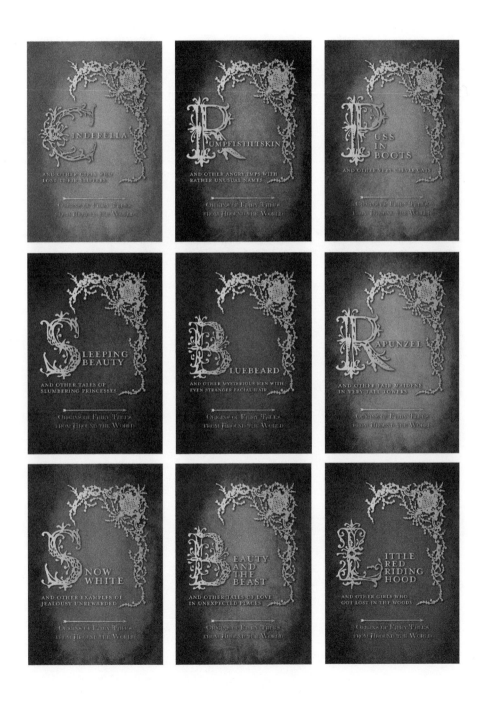

Cinderella
AND OTHER GIRLS WHO
LOST THEIR SLIPPERS

Origins of Fairy Tales
from Around the World

Rumpelstiltskin
AND OTHER ANGRY IMPS WITH
RATHER UNUSUAL NAMES

Origins of Fairy Tales
from Around the World

Puss in Boots
AND OTHER VERY CLEVER CATS

Origins of Fairy Tales
from Around the World

Sleeping Beauty
AND OTHER TALES OF
SLUMBERING PRINCESSES

Origins of Fairy Tales
from Around the World

Bluebeard
AND OTHER MYSTERIOUS MEN WITH
EVEN STRANGER FACIAL HAIR

Origins of Fairy Tales
from Around the World

Rapunzel
AND OTHER FAIR MAIDENS
IN VERY TALL TOWERS

Origins of Fairy Tales
from Around the World

Snow White
AND OTHER EXAMPLES OF
JEALOUSY UNREWARDED

Origins of Fairy Tales
from Around the World

Beauty and the Beast
AND OTHER TALES OF LOVE
IN UNEXPECTED PLACES

Origins of Fairy Tales
from Around the World

Little Red Riding Hood
AND OTHER GIRLS WHO
GOT LOST IN THE WOODS

Origins of Fairy Tales
from Around the World

Lightning Source UK Ltd.
Milton Keynes UK
UKHW050027210519
342994UK00006B/55/P